Rockets

MY SISTER'S NAME IS **ROVER**

Rover's Birthday

Chris Powling and Scoular Anderson

A & C Black • London

Rockets

ROVER - Chris Powling and Scoular Anderson

Rover's Birthday
Rover the Champion
Rover Goes to School
Rover Shows Off

First paperback edition 2000
First published 1999 in hardback by
A & C Black (Publishers) Ltd
35 Bedford Row, London WC1R 4JH

Text copyright © 1999 Chris Powling
Illustrations copyright © 1999 Scoular Anderson

The right of Chris Powling and Scoular Anderson
to be identified as author and illustrator of this work
has been asserted by them in accordance with
the Copyright, Designs and Patents Act 1988.

ISBN 0-7136-5199-7

A CIP catalogue record for this book is available
from the British Library.

Printed and bound by G. Z. Printek, Bilbao, Spain.

My sister's name is Rover.

Yes, I know that's a name you give to a puppy. A yappy, happy, roly-poly puppy is what my sister would love to be.

'Puppies have a lot more fun than girls do,' she always says.

'Do you really think so?' asked Granpa, one Saturday morning.

Yes, I do. I wish I was a puppy all the time.

And to prove it, the only things she wanted for her birthday were doggy things.

But I was blowed if I was going to buy her anything to do with dogs. She was bad enough already.

I could still remember the weekend when she first became a kind of puppy. This was when Granpa made the puppy costume.

He used to be chief
costume-maker at a
big London theatre.
So I should have
guessed it would be
brilliant.

Well, it was brilliant.

Sara turned into Rover as soon as she
saw it. And she's been Rover ever since.

Maybe this birthday was her last chance to start being a girl again. So I took no notice of all the doggy hints she dropped.

My present would be *sensible*.

At last her birthday arrived. It began the way all birthdays do in our house – with a special breakfast for the birthday puppy – sorry, person.

11

Dad carried my sister's cards to the table in his mouth as if he were a puppy himself.

'Good boy! Good boy!' she giggled as she patted him on the head.

Then, growling to herself, she opened the envelopes.

Honestly, nearly every card had some sort of dog on it – an Alsatian, a spaniel, a terrier, a Labrador.

There was even a musical dog on Granpa's.

Only one card was different. My card.
This had a picture of a
cat instead.

Big mistake.

My sister pretended to chase it all over
the room as if it were a real cat.

Everyone laughed at this except me.
Mind you, that's what you get if your
mum and dad are actors.

Now it was time to open the presents. My sister stuck out her tongue and panted – huh-huh, huh-huh, huh-huh. She reminded me of a dog that's over-excited.

'I hope you like them,' Dad winked.
'Woof!' said my sister.

He'd bought her a pair of dog bowls –
one for eating and one for drinking.
Both were printed with a name:

I began to feel a bit uneasy.

Mum's present came next.

My sister's eyes lit up when she
unwrapped it. 'A collar and lead,'
she exclaimed.

You can guess the name on the tag.

Now I felt really uncomfortable.

Then she picked up my present. By now
I was starting to panic.

To tell the truth I wanted to forget my present altogether.

You see, it was really boring. I'd got it from the junk shop down in the village. It was supposed to help my sister keep her dressing-up clothes tidy – so they weren't scattered all over her bedroom.

Now I wished I'd bought her something doggy after all.

No one noticed the look on my face, though. Granpa's present had everyone paying attention... even me.

We all gasped when my sister pulled it out of its wrapping paper.

Wow!

It was the biggest
and best book about
dogs I'd ever seen.

Why hadn't I
bought a puppy-
present like
everyone else?

It was far too late for that though.
I watched miserably as my sister
performed her puppy tricks.

'Catch this, Rover!' said Dad, tossing her a biscuit.

You can bet my sister did everything
they asked.

You can bet she did it
brilliantly as well.

She was that kind of kid. Or do I mean
that kind of dog? I didn't care which it
was as long as she forgot there was one
more present.

My present.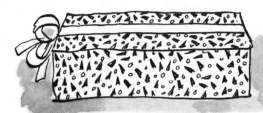

A present that was amazingly BORING.

For a while I thought I was safe till I saw Mum suddenly frown.

I snatched up my birthday card from the floor and rushed outside.

I ran round the garden, skipping just ahead of her. This was easy because I was on two legs and she was on four.

It was a lot of fun, I admit.

Especially when grumpy Mrs Robinson from next door peered over our fence.

'It's not an animal,' I tried to explain.

Mrs Robinson stared at my sister.

She disappeared
so quickly, you'd
have thought
Rover had been
chasing her.

That was the end of our game, though. We could hear Granpa calling from the back step.

But it was too late. She was already lolloping up the garden path.

By the time I got back inside, my present was nearly unwrapped.

I shuddered when at last she pulled out the big, old, wickerwork basket from the junk shop.

It was just the right size and shape for all her dressing-up clothes.

So *sensible.*

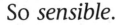

Rover stared at it without a word...
or without a bark, rather. Her eyes,
when she looked at me, were big and
bright and puppy-like.

'It's perfect!' she howled.

Rover had curled up in it, you see.

There she lay, all cosy and puppyish,
with her snout hanging over one side
and her tail hanging over the other.

She gave a little puppy sigh
of happiness.

The End